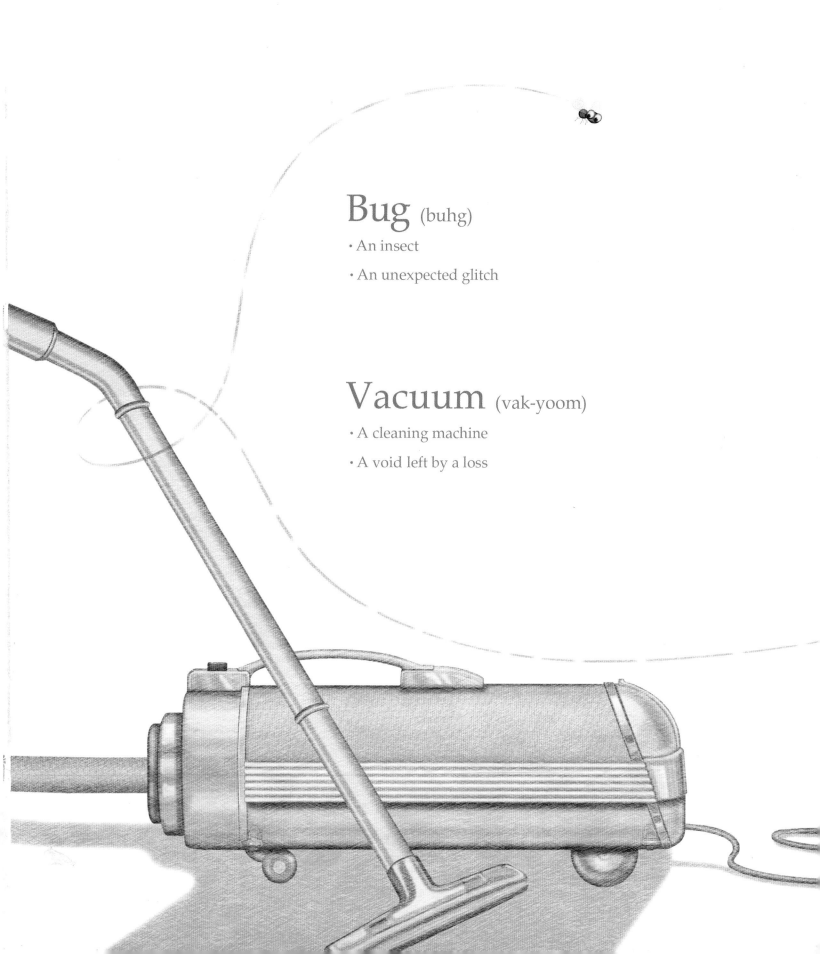

Bug (buhg)

· An insect

· An unexpected glitch

Vacuum (vak-yoom)

· A cleaning machine

· A void left by a loss

For Granny, Gaëtan, Gigi, Gilles and Louise

BUG
in a
VACUUM

Written and illustrated by
Mélanie Watt

TUNDRA BOOKS

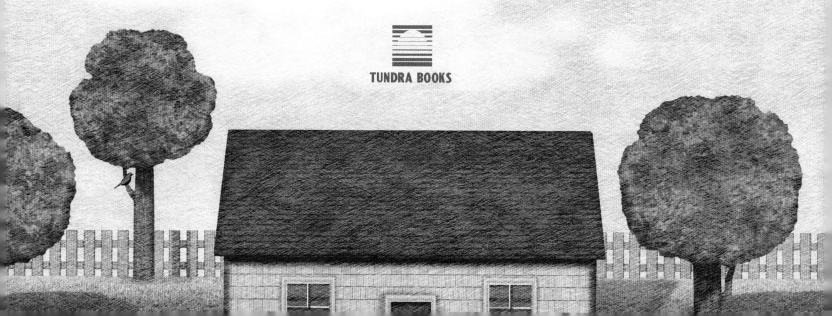

The bug started here.

It flew into the house …

NEW!

WASH AWAY THE DIRT!

POUR HERE.

Bubble Soap

Ready for clean clothes?
Want brighter whites?
Need noticeable results?

Cold
Warm
Hot

Buzzed through the bathroom …

Zigzagged across a bedroom ...

And stopped.

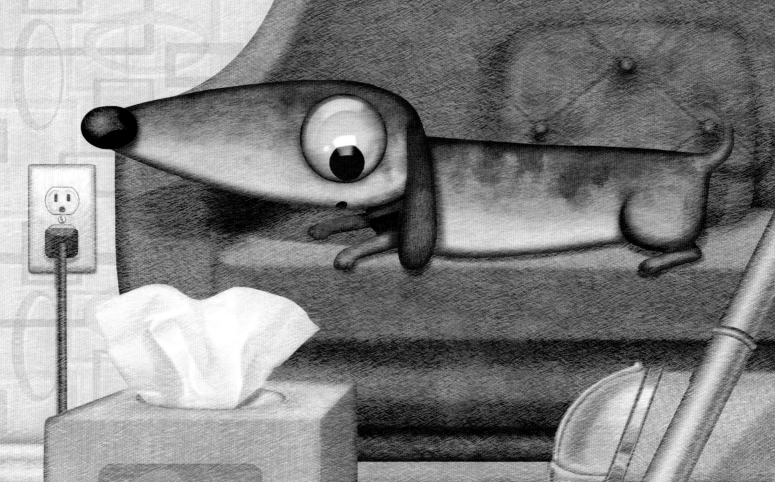

It was on top of the world
when it happened.

Its entire life changed with
the switch of a button.

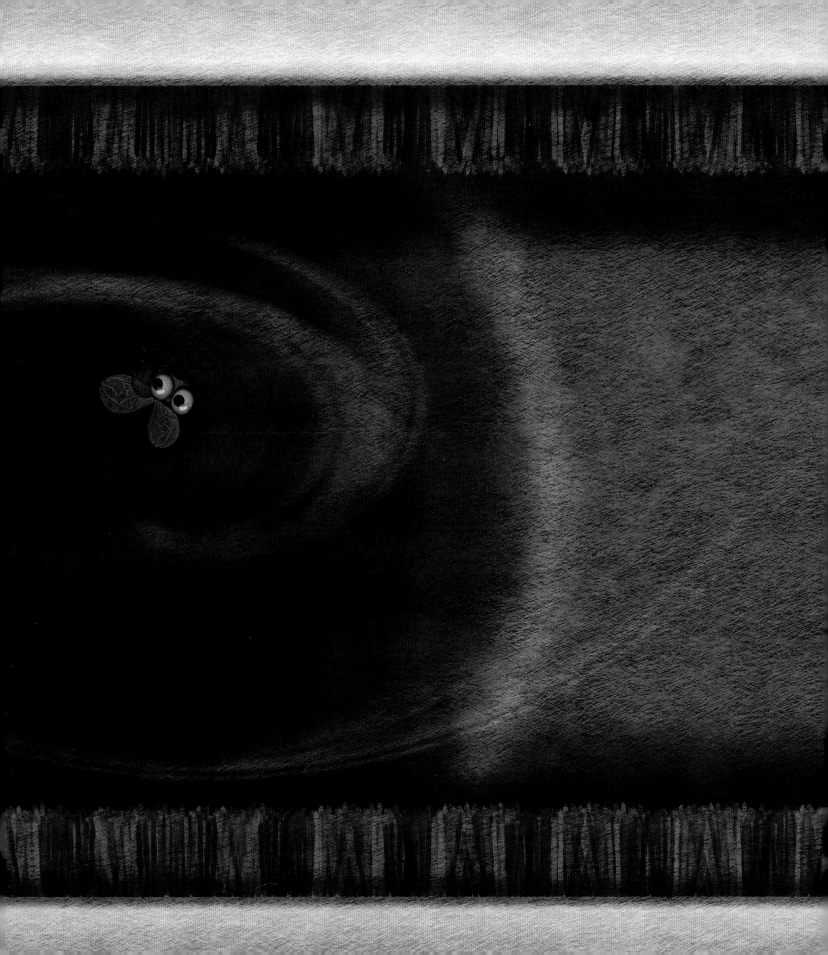

Where am I?

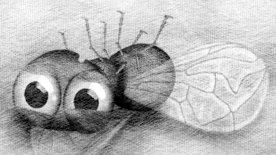

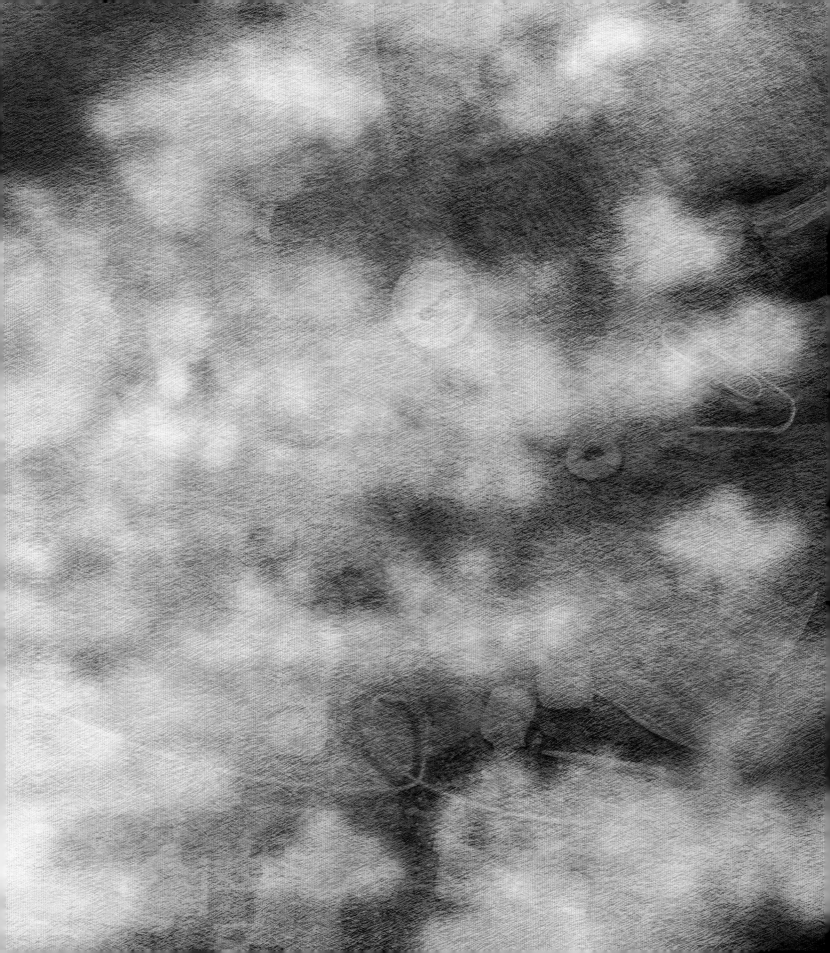

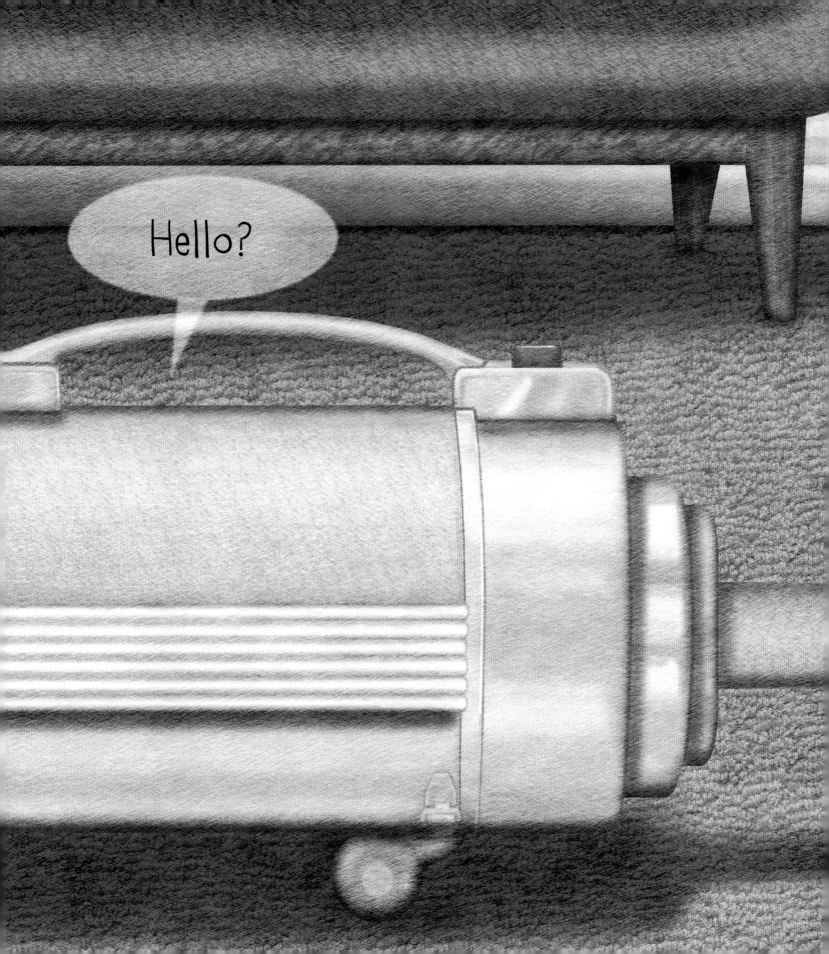

Stage One

This is
amazing!

Doesn't get
much cozier
than this ...

Can't wait to
tell my friends about
this place!

But something's fishy—
the lights are out and
it's awfully quiet ...

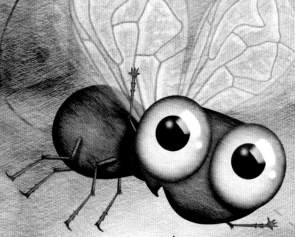

Could this be ...
a surprise
party?

Dream!
I'll pinch myself
and wake up ...

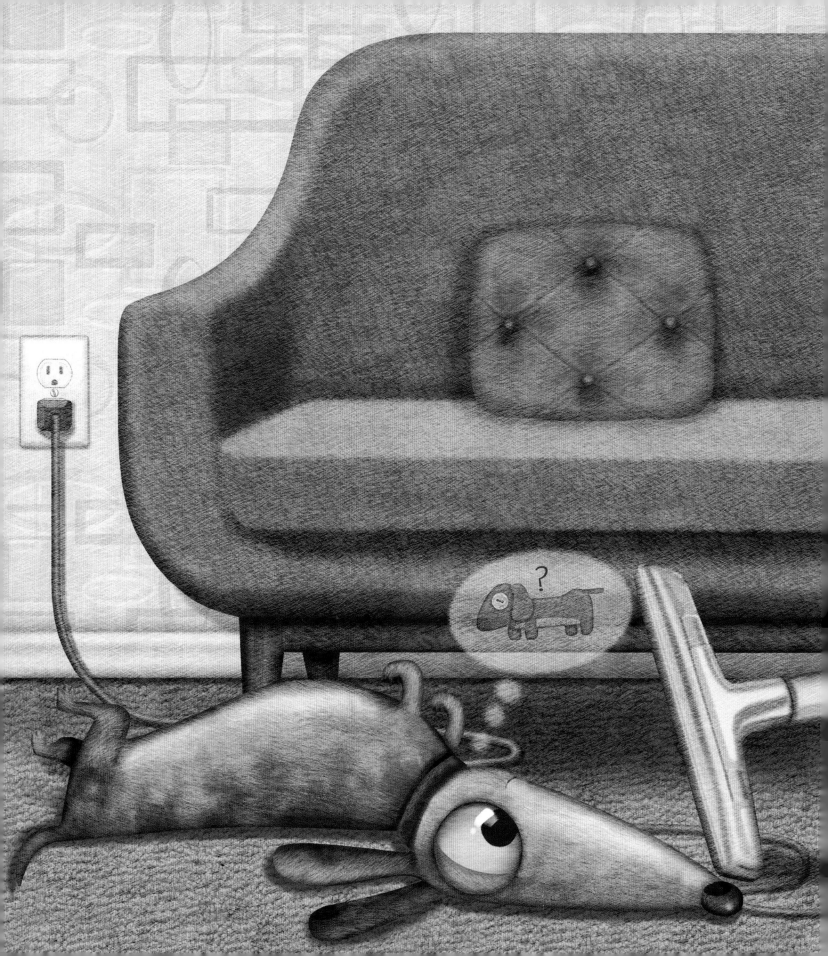

Stage Two

A NEW YOU!
WASH AWAY YOUR TROUBLES!
POUR YOUR HEART OUT HERE.
Bargaining
Ready for a clean slate?
Want a brighter future?
Need results fast?

Tonight's bowling night with the dung beetles!

Stage Three

FIGHT BACK!
ANGER
Ingredients:
A spoonful of bitterness, a scoop of bad temper and a pinch of revenge
HOW TO SERVE:
Stir it around and fire it up!
QUICK & MESSY

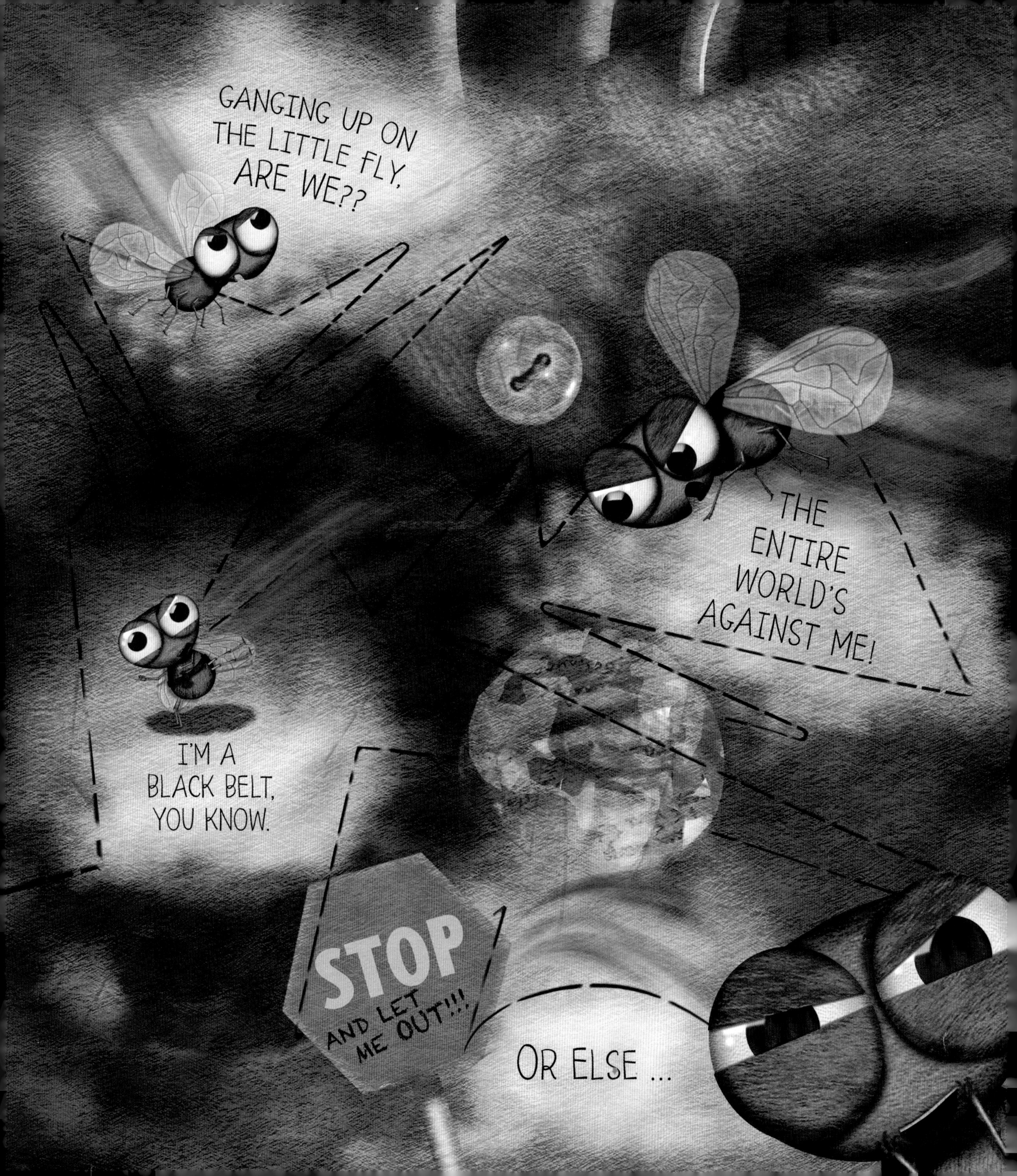
GANGING UP ON THE LITTLE FLY, ARE WE??
THE ENTIRE WORLD'S AGAINST ME!
I'M A BLACK BELT, YOU KNOW.
STOP
AND LET ME OUT!!!
OR ELSE ...

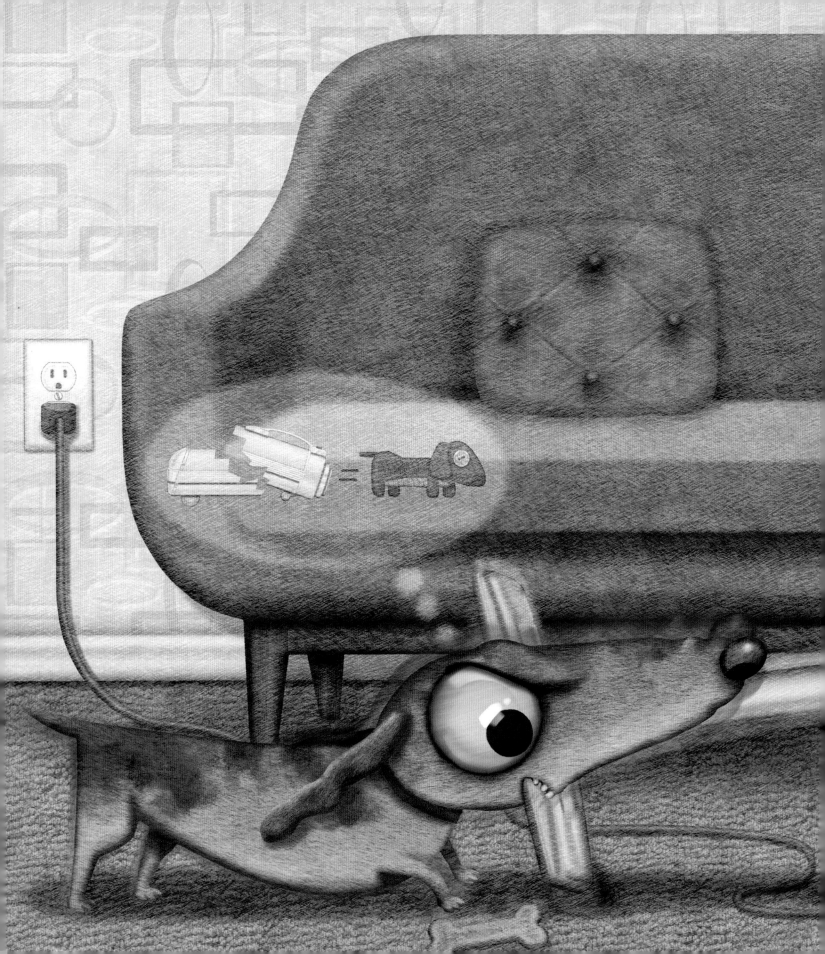

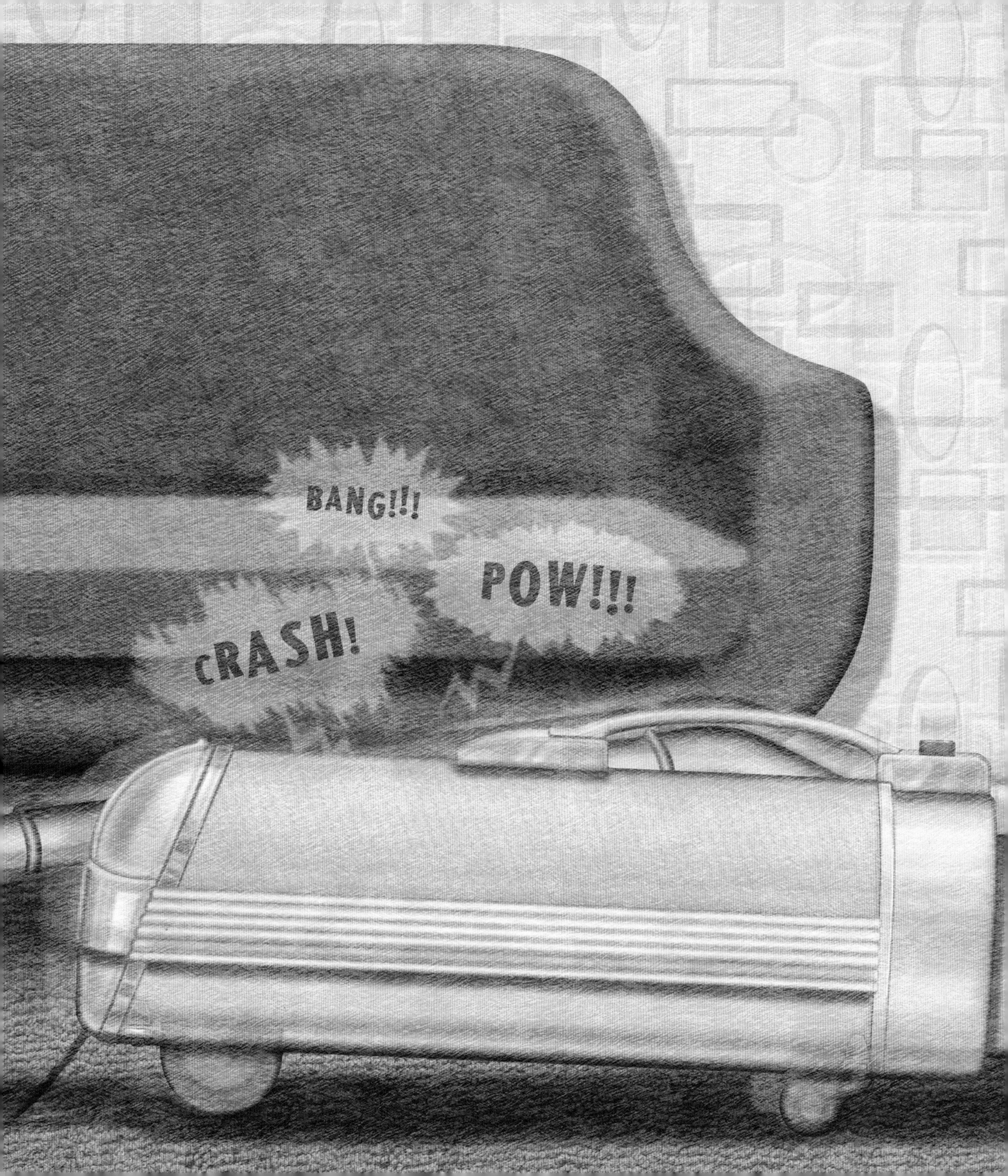
BANG!!!
POW!!!
CRASH!

Stage Four

DESPAIR
DESPAIR
An Unfair Tale with an Unhappy Ending
Based on a truly SAD story

I'm at the end of my rope.
No light at the end of the tunnel.
The odds are against me.
My dreams are crushed!!!

I'll never see the sky again.

I'll **never** be extraordinary.

I'll **never** visit new places.

Let's face it ...

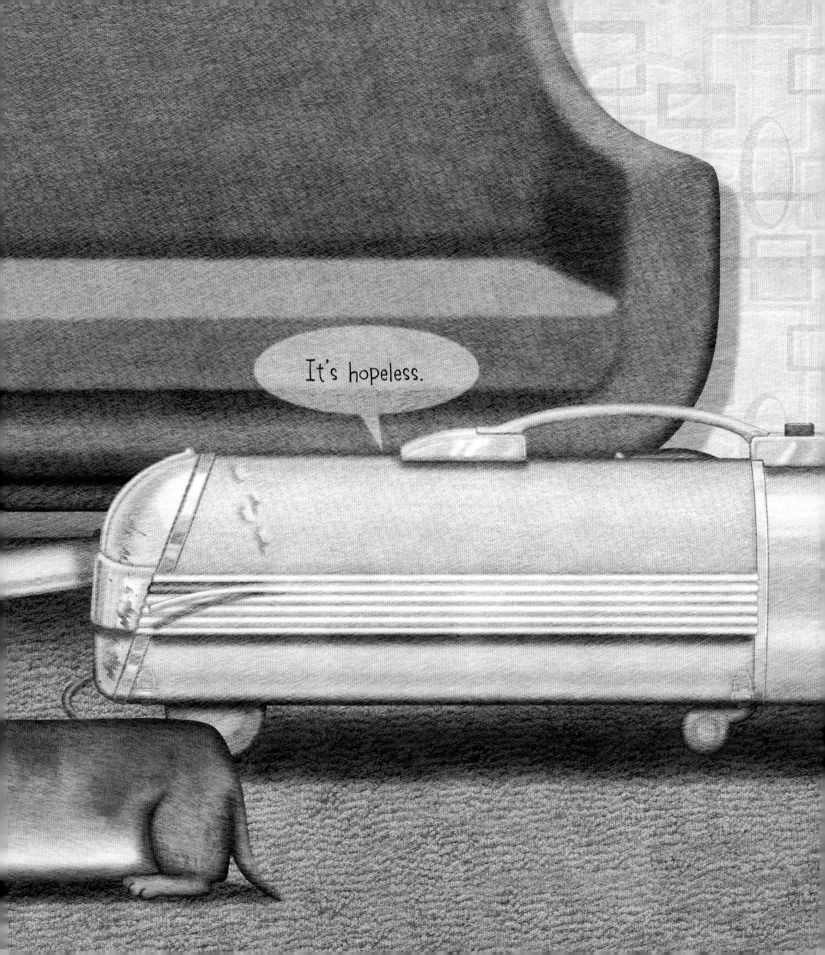

Stage Five

Acceptance
Gentle and comforting
No regrets
100% Real Feelings

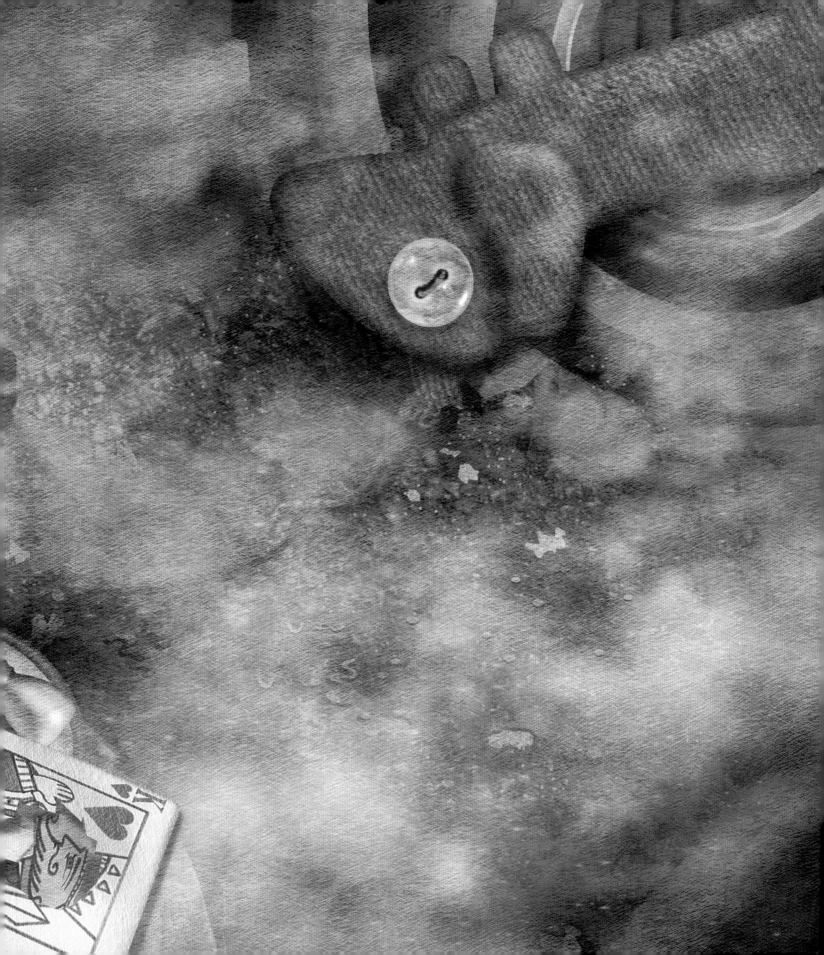

I'll let my imagination fly.

I'll appreciate what I have.

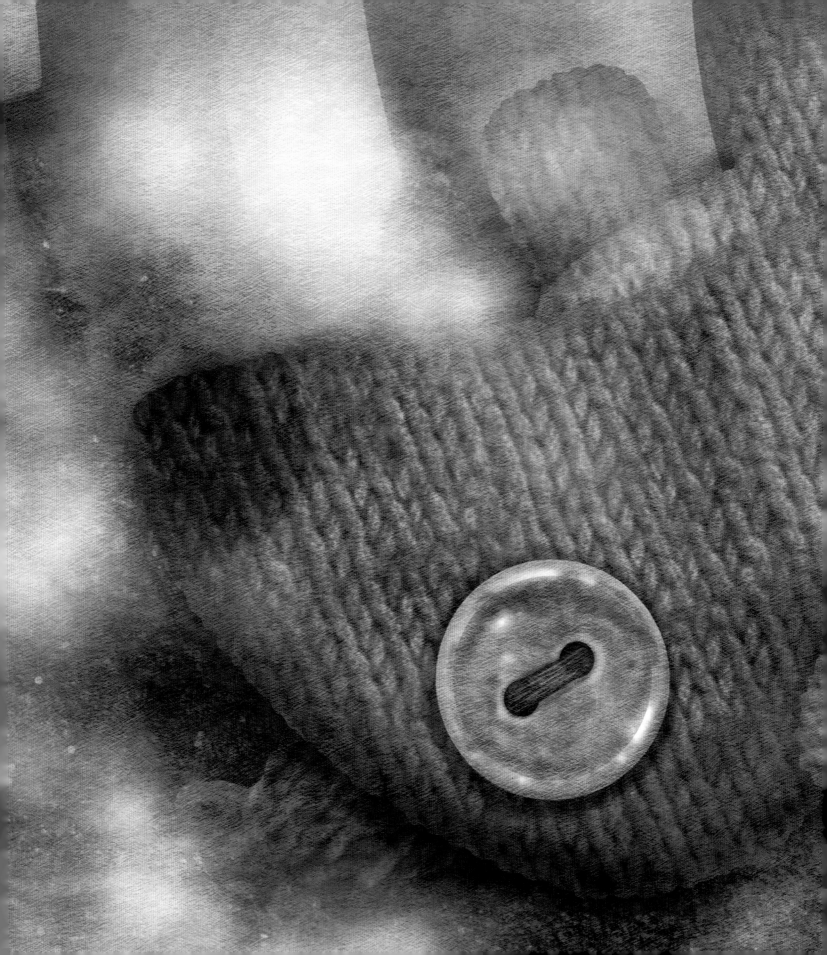

Thanks
for lending
an ear, pal.

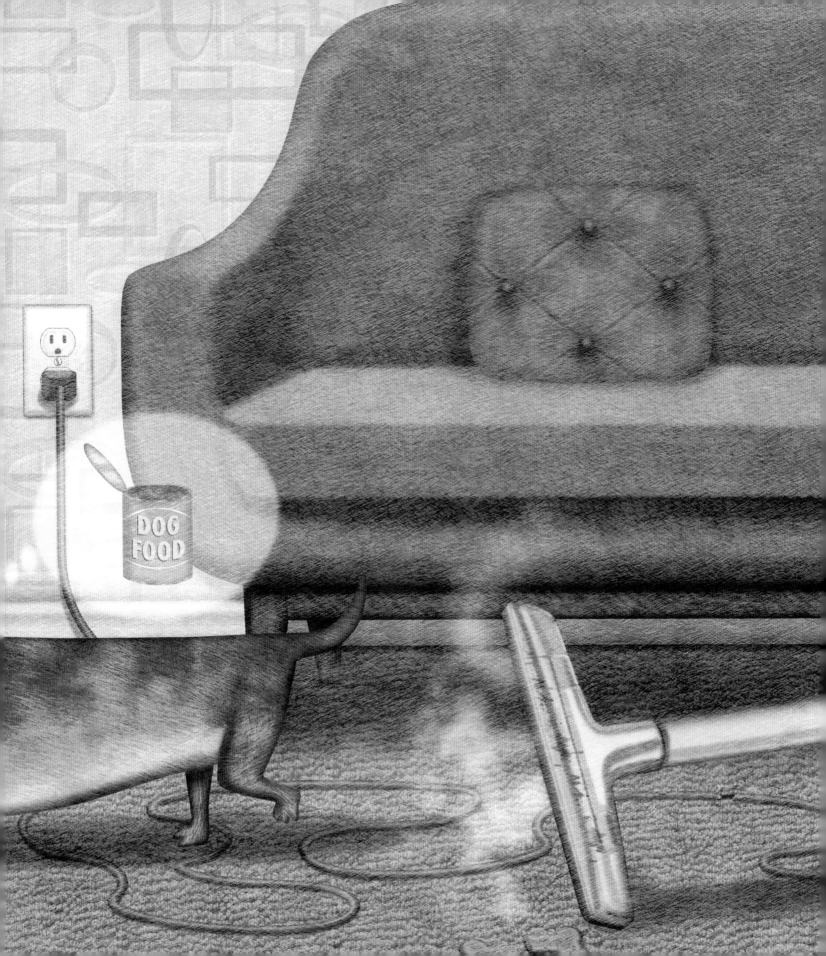

DOG
FOOD

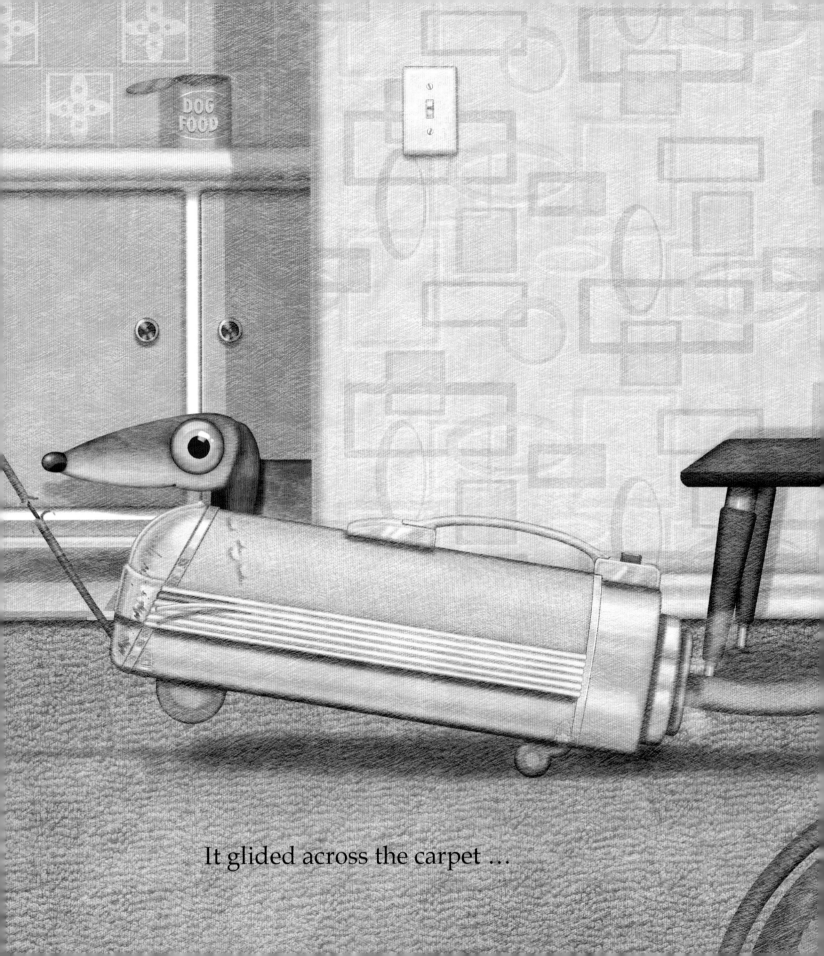

It glided across the carpet …

Waited at the curb …

Traveled down the street …

Continued up the hills …

Fell into a heap …

And stopped.

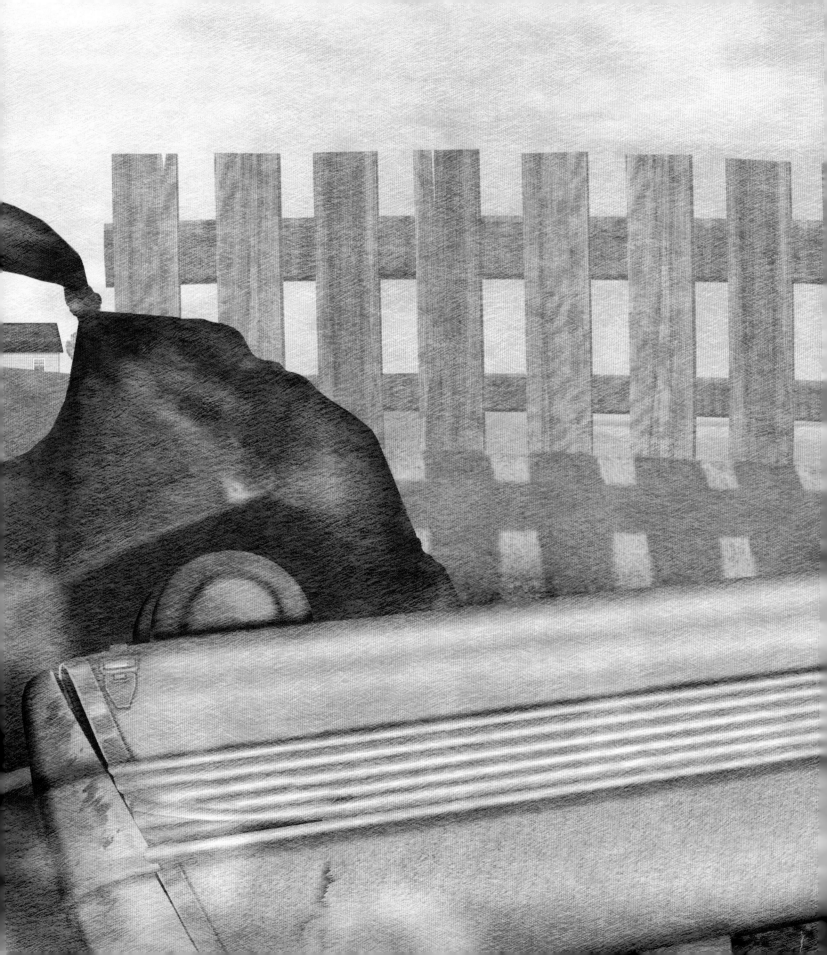

And the bug started here.

The five stages of grief,
also known as the Kübler-Ross
model, introduced in 1969, are
a series of emotions commonly
experienced when facing a
life-changing event.

Text and illustrations copyright © 2015 by Mélanie Watt

Published in Canada and the United States of America by Tundra Books,
a division of Random House of Canada Limited,
a Penguin Random House Company

Library of Congress Control Number: 2014951818

Library and Archives Canada Cataloguing in Publication

Watt, Mélanie, 1975-, author
Bug in a vacuum / written and illustrated by Mélanie Watt.

Issued in print and electronic formats.
ISBN 978-1-77049-645-3 (bound).—ISBN 978-1-77049-647-7 (epub)

I. Title.

PS8645.A884B83 2015   jC813'.6   C2014-903050-9
                                                C2014-903051-7

Edited by Tara Walker. Designed by Mélanie Watt
The artwork in this book was rendered in mixed media.

www.tundrabooks.com
www.penguinrandomhouse.ca

Printed and bound in China

1 2 3 4 5 6   20 19 18 17 16 15

TUNDRA BOOKS | Penguin Random House